CONTENTS

COLOUR FIRST READER books are perfect for beginner readers. All the text inside this Colour First Reader book has been checked and approved by a reading specialist, so it is the ideal size, length and level for children learning to read.

Series Reading Consultant: Prue Goodwin
Reading and Language Information Centre,
University of Reading

THE GHOST TEACHER

TONY BRADMAN
Illustrated by Peter Kavanagh

www.kidsatrandomhouse.co.uk

Shiver One

This is Sunny Bank Infant and Junior.

It looks like an ordinary school . . . It certainly *sounds* like an ordinary school . . . It smells like an ordinary school too, all musty and dusty and chalky, with wandering whiffs of school dinners and of disinfectant.

And that's mostly what it is —
an ordinary school, a very
ordinary school indeed. But wait …
something *EXTRA*-ordinary is
about to happen here. Something
very strange, and very peculiar,
and very, very … *SPOOKY*!

Look … there by the dustbins,
what do you see? A shimmering
and a glimmering, and a figure
forming in the darkness.

It is The Ghost Teacher, and her name is Miss Shade.

She glides over to a window, and peers in . . .

"Class Three! *Class Three!*" Somebody was trying hard to make herself heard above an absolutely terrible din. "Will you *please* be quiet and behave! I'm warning you, this is *definitely* your last chance . . ."

"Oh dear, things are much, much worse than I thought," whispered Miss Shade. "I only hope I'm not too late ..."

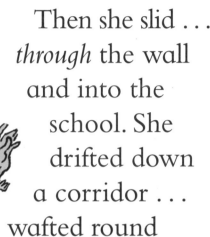

Then she slid ... *through* the wall and into the school. She drifted down a corridor ... wafted round a corner ... then slipped through a keyhole. She was in the classroom where the absolutely terrible din was coming from.

No one there could see her . . .
not yet, anyway. But she could
see them. And Class Three were
doing what they did best –
behaving badly.

They got up to the usual things, of course – dreaming when they should be working,

fidgeting when they should be sitting still,

chattering when they should be listening,

picking their noses and flicking it at each other.

They did much more, though.

They did lots
of pulling and
prodding
and poking.

They did lots
of crashing and
bashing and
practical joking.

They did lots
of fighting
and biting
and writing . . .

but only
on the wall.

This is what Class Three's classroom looked like at nine o'clock on the first morning of term.

This is what it looked like just *one hour* later.

And this is . . . what Class Three look like. They're shocking, aren't they?

Class Three made more noise than the rest of Sunny Bank Infant and Junior School put together. They were more trouble than a barrel full of babies. In short, Class Three were . . . a teacher's worst nightmare.

This is Miss Nicely, Class Three's teacher. She was trying to do what *she* did best – teaching Class Three all sorts of interesting stuff.

But Class Three, as usual, weren't taking any notice of her. And Miss Nicely was feeling fed up. She was fed up with shouting. She was fed up with not being listened to. She was very fed up with Class Three.

This is what Miss Nicely looked like at nine o'clock on the first morning of term.

This is what she looked like just *one hour* later.

And this is an extreme close-up of what she looks like today. It's shocking, isn't it?

Suddenly, something snapped inside her.

Right, Class Three, that's it!

She grabbed her handbag and headed towards the door. For once, Class Three *did* take notice. "Hey, Miss!" they called out rudely. "Where are you going?"

Then she slammed the door shut behind her, and strode off down the corridor. Miss Shade slid through the classroom wall, and wafted along after Miss Nicely. They could both hear Class Three . . . cheering.

This is
Mr Dickens,
headteacher
of Sunny
Bank Infant
and Junior.

He looks like an ordinary
headteacher. He sounds like an
ordinary headteacher. He smells
like an ordinary headteacher too,
all musty and dusty and chalky,
with wandering whiffs of school
dinners and disinfectant.

And that's exactly what he is,
an ordinary headteacher, a very
ordinary headteacher indeed.
At that precise moment he was
*head*ing down the corridor too,
and he was about to bump into
Miss Nicely.

"Not any more, there isn't," said Miss Nicely. "I resign, Mr Dickens. You can find somebody else to be Class Three's teacher from now on."

And with that, she swept out of the school.

A horrified Mr Dickens watched her go. He listened to Class Three creating havoc in the distance, and a frown crossed his face. Then he turned and marched off to his office, looking very, *very* ... determined.

"Umm," murmured Miss Shade. "Time I got to work ..."

Miss Shade glided along the corridor to Class Three's classroom, where the din was even more terrible than before. She waited outside for a moment, listening and tutting. Then she slid in through the . . . *closed* door.

And this time she made sure everyone there could see her.

Class Three were rather surprised by her ... *appearance*. In fact, they were so surprised, they stopped having a riot. They went very quiet indeed.

This is what they looked like before Miss Shade appeared.

And this is what they looked
like *one second* later. They froze
in the middle of whatever
naughtiness they were up to.

They look shocked, don't they?
"Good morning, Class Three,"

said Miss Shade. Class Three
didn't reply, although some of
them did close their mouths. "My
name is Miss Shade, and I will
be standing in for Miss Nicely.
We've got lots to do so . . ."

Are you a ... g-g-g-ghost, Miss?

said somebody brave.

"Of course I am!" said Miss Shade. There was a sharp intake of breath from the entire class. "Now, settle down, everybody," continued Miss Shade. "I'm going to ..."

The entire class trembled ...

...tell you a story.

Class Three
stopped trembling,
and breathed out
in relief.

What k-k-k-kind
of story, Miss?

said the brave child.

A ... scary one.
Are you ready?

She clicked her ghostly fingers,
and it went dark. Strange,
haunting noises filled the air.
Peculiar wisps of light
appeared from everywhere.
  And Miss Shade gave off
a . . . *spooky* glow.

"N-n-n-no we're not!"

everybody in Class Three wailed. They hugged each other in fright, but Miss Shade took absolutely no notice of them.

"Once upon a time," she said, in a voice that made the little hairs stand up on the backs of the children's necks, "there was a school, a very ordinary school.

But in that school there was a badly behaved class . . ."

As Class Three watched, the wall behind Miss Shade turned blurry, began to fade, then vanished completely. A phantom classroom appeared, and with a gasp, Class Three recognized the people in it straight away.

"Hey, *that's us!*" they yelled,
amazed.

"In fact, they were absolutely
awful," continued Miss Shade.
"They never allowed their poor,
poor teacher a moment's peace.
They misbehaved the whole time.
And I'm sorry to say they did
some *terrible* things . . ."

The phantom classroom before Class Three wobbled, and changed. Soon Class Three were watching something like a film on fast forward. And they saw everything they had got up to since the first day of term.

They saw all the pulling and prodding and poking. They saw all the crashing and bashing and practical joking. They saw all the fighting and biting. And they definitely saw all the writing on the wall.

None of them said a word. But as they sat there in the darkness watching themselves, some of Class Three *did* feel slightly ... ashamed.

Their poor, poor teacher always tried hard to make the lessons interesting.

The phantom film slowed,
then cut to a vision of Miss
Nicely working at home.

"But the class didn't give a hoot."

Now some more of Class Three
felt quite . . . ashamed.

"Then one day," said Miss Shade, "the class behaved *so* badly, their poor, poor teacher couldn't stand it a minute longer. She left, and started looking for another job, any job . . . provided it didn't involve children."

At last, the whole of Class Three felt very ashamed indeed. Although that didn't stop one or two of them from still being rather . . . cheeky.

"Here, Miss!" a voice called out. "This story isn't very scary!"

"Don't worry," said Miss Shade. "We're just getting to the scary part ... The head of the school had to find someone to replace the poor, poor teacher.

So he decided to put an advertisement in the newspaper."

The vision of Miss Nicely wobbled, and changed into a picture of Mr Dickens writing at his desk:

NEW TEACHER WANTED AT SUNNY BANK SCHOOL MUST BE VERY, VERY, VERY STRICT.

Mr Dickens

Then the phantom picture went into fast forward again.

Class Three watched as the newspaper was printed, teachers read the advertisement and replied, then came to be interviewed for the job by Mr Dickens. "Finally, the head found the person he was looking for," said Miss Shade. "Someone who would keep you under control, someone who wouldn't stand for any nonsense. In short, Class Three – your worst nightmare . . ." Class Three gulped at the vision before them.

Shiver Three

It was a teacher with a beaky nose and an even beakier chin. It was a teacher with a tight little bun and an even tighter little mouth. It was a teacher with steely blue eyes that saw ... *everything*.

And her name was ... *Miss Stern*. A phone rang in the phantom film. Miss Stern reached out and answered it. Her voice made Class Three instantly sit up straight.

Miss Stern put the phone down, and slowly turned to stare at Class Three. The phantom film froze with her eyes drilling into them. A few of the children – probably the cheeky ones – let slip little moans.

"Please, Miss, tell us it isn't true!"

"I only wish I could," said Miss Shade sadly. "But alas, I can't. You have seen your past, Class Three, and what is happening in the present. You have also seen your future, and that cannot be changed. Unless ..."

"Unless what, Miss?" several voices called out eagerly.

"Unless," said Miss Shade, "you change . . . *yourselves*. You *could* give up the pulling and prodding and poking, the crashing and bashing and practical joking, and the fighting and biting and writing on the wall . . ."

"We can't!" said a voice. "We *love* doing that stuff! It's what we do best, isn't it, everybody?"

There was much murmuring of agreement.

"Oh well," said Miss Shade with a sigh.

"If that's the way you feel, I won't argue. But you'd better get used to how things are going to be . . ." Miss Shade clicked her ghostly fingers.

Suddenly Miss Stern's phantom film face came to life once more.

"Right, Class Three!" she snapped. "Silence! No play time until you've finished all the difficult sums …"

"OK, we surrender!" yelled Class Three, remembering too the shame they'd felt at seeing what they'd done. "Please help us to get Miss Nicely back," one of them added. "We'll do *anything* you say."

"Cross your hearts and hope to die?" asked Miss Shade.

"If we don't, we'll eat worm pie!" chanted Class Three.

"I'm glad to hear it," said Miss Shade, clicking her ghostly fingers again. The darkness was replaced by light, and the wall returned to normal. "Right, you can make a start by tidying this classroom. It's a *disgrace* . . ." Class Three set to work with a will.

This is what the classroom
looked like when they began.

This is what it looked like just
one hour later.

And this is Class Three looking a bit shocked at being so well behaved.

"What do you think, Miss?" said somebody proudly.

"I think you never know what you can do until you've tried, Class Three," replied Miss Shade. "Wouldn't you agree? Now I want you all to sit down, fold your arms, and prepare to say something very important."

Miss Shade clicked her fingers one last time. Soft, sprinkly, tinkling sounds came from everywhere, and then . . . a dazed Miss Nicely appeared out of thin air. Miss Shade made sure Miss Nicely couldn't see her.

"Oh, no," Miss Nicely groaned, and closed her eyes. "I can't stand it!"

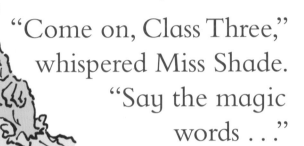

"Come on, Class Three," whispered Miss Shade. "Say the magic words . . ."

"*Sorry*, Miss Nicely!" said someone. Other voices joined in, and soon the whole of Class Three was apologizing.

Miss Nicely
opened her eyes.
She looked as if
she'd just woken
from her worst
nightmare. She
smiled faintly.

Then Mr Dickens came in.

"Ah, you're back, Miss Nicely," he said, and dropped a crumpled piece of paper in the bin. "I see you've got everything under control here too. Nicely done, Miss Nicely. Keep up the good work, Class Three!"

"I couldn't have put it better myself," whispered Miss Shade. She smiled, waved goodbye . . . and slipped out through the keyhole.

"Who said that?" asked Mr Dickens.

But nobody told him . . .

That's more or less the end of this story. Class Three *did* keep up the good work, except for some dreaming and fidgeting and chattering and nose picking and flicking. Miss Nicely didn't mind all that, though.

She wasn't *quite* sure what had happened. But compared to how they'd been before, Class Three were . . . *angels*, so she wasn't complaining.

And what, you ask, became of Miss Shade? Well, as long as there's a class misbehaving somewhere, there's no rest for The Ghost Teacher.

Which means the next school
to get a SPOOKY visit is . . .
BOUND TO BE YOURS!